Dating the Damsel

ENCHANTED WISHES COLLECTION

VIOLA TEMPEST

VIOLA TEMPEST PUBLISHING

Copyright

Dating the Damsel
Enchanted Wishes Collection

© Copyright 2023 Viola Tempest

Cover Design by Fay Lane Cover Design

Contents

Dating the Damsel

ENCHANTED WISHES COLLECTION

VIOLA TEMPEST

Chapter One

Scarlett ran through the front door, tears streaming down her face, before throwing herself onto the couch. I jumped at her entrance, but at the sight and sound of the sobs racking through her small body, my muscles relaxed. I let out a slow sigh before getting up, nudging the front door closed, and making my way over to her trembling form, curled on the couch cushions.

I nudged her hand with my wet nose until it rested across my neck. I let out a low grumble, trying to get her to look at me. *Scarlett*, I grumbled, *look at me, please.* At times like this, I wish more than anything that I could soothe her with words that she would understand.

Sobs racked Scarlett's small frame. Her thin shoulders shook as short gasps clawed out from her throat. The congestion in her throat and her nose were audible. She had been crying for some time. That thought made my chest tighten and squeeze even more. I nudged her hair away from her downturned face, sniffling in her ear. She normally swatted me away for blowing air into her ears, her smile full of laughs and teasing. But this time, her sobs only slowed slightly.

She sniffled as she turned her head toward me. Her eyes glistened with tears, the skin around them red and puffy. God, this one wasn't good. I knew she shouldn't have gone on that date. That boy was trouble from the beginning. I knew he would let her down. I knew it, and yet I could do nothing to stop her from going.

I swallowed as she met my gaze with trembling lips and tears stained on her rosy cheeks.

"Why does this always happen to me, Kadri?" She whimpered. "Why do I always pick the bad ones?"

I extended my snout and nudged her cheek, pushing aside more wet hair. She sniffled, but let me nuzzle her. Good, she wasn't pushing me away. She was saddened—but not angry this time.

I eyed her, letting her catch her breath before I tilted my head. *What happened?* I wanted to ask. But she always seemed to understand me, even if I couldn't speak to her in her own tongue.

She let out a shuddering breath. "He was late. I arrived at the café, ordered a coffee, and sat at a table waiting for him for over an hour. I got all dolled up, and while I was waiting, I did my makeup all cute. I even did my hair for him!"

I nodded slowly. She liked to dress up, and she liked to appear cute and pretty on a daily basis. But her long, crimson hair, hanging nearly to her hips, was a whole other story. She usually threw it into a bun or a ponytail just to get it out of the way.

I had laid my body on the floor just outside the bathroom mere hours ago while she sang to her favorite songs that blared from the radio, while painstakingly curling and bouncing her hair. She left the house in a flowy red sundress that shined against her fair skin, black wedges to add some height to her small form, a bag full of makeup to paint her face with because she always got to these dates early, and red curls bouncing around her shoulders. She had grinned at me as she left, that hopeful, eager smile gleaming. Now, it was a wobbly, tearful mess.

I lifted a paw and gently laid it atop her hand. She smiled tightly and brushed a thumb over my fur, but the curl of her lips was forced.

"I got there early like I always do, did my makeup,

drank my coffee, and even read through a magazine that was on the table. But then ten o'clock came and went, and Logan didn't come." She sniffled. "I thought he might not show, but then almost an hour and fifteen minutes later, he rushed through the door. And I-I was so happy that he even came at all that I shrugged off his tardiness."

I kept her gaze even if I wanted to shake my head. She shouldn't have stayed. She shouldn't have waited for a man who didn't respect her time or commitment. That was a red flag—why did she always ignore those?

"He apologized over and over, saying he had car trouble and had to take his bike instead, and I just waved him off. It was fine, and things happen. No big deal. I was just happy that he came at all, and we could hang out and enjoy our time together."

But...

"Things were good at first. He ordered a coffee and a sandwich, we talked and joked, and he told me about the upcoming vacation he planned to go on with his friends. Apparently, his guy friends and himself were planning to go to the islands for a long weekend. They were going to rent hotel rooms and already had everything lined up in their itinerary. And then he said his friends were all going to bring a girl with them. Some had girlfriends while others were bringing hookups or even just casual female friends."

Ah, I nodded in understanding. *This is where it all went wrong.*

Scarlett sniffled, a harsh sob choking her. But she pushed on through her tears and wobbly voice.

"It all sounded so luxurious and fun and—you know, I haven't been to the islands before. So, I asked him if he was bringing a girl, too. He said he was, but he still had to ask if she wanted to come. We had been on four dates, and his smile at me made me all warm and mushy inside. He had to ask me to come, right? Of course, he'd ask me."

Scarlett's composure snapped as a sob raked through her. "No. He didn't want to ask me to come on this luxurious vacation. He didn't want to ask if I was even interested. He only wanted to meet up today to tell me that he was going on this vacation with another girl, who, apparently, he has been seeing recently. One whom he has gone on two dates with and *really feels a connection with*."

Oh, no... Scarlett—

Tears streamed down her cheeks as her nose leaked. She gasped for breath as choking sobs coursed through her. I turned for only a moment to pick up a tissue box with my mouth. I set it in front of her and nudged her hand to grab a tissue. She did and blew into the fabric with the force of a trumpet. I flinched.

"Logan dumped me. Just flat out dumped me for this new girl whom he has already decided is 'the one' and wants to go on this trip with instead. And then... and then..." She choked on a forced breath. I leaned my furry head on her hand and urged her to finish.

"And then he just got up and left, leaving me to pay for his meal, too. And the icing on the cake? The girl he's seeing picked him up in her car. Yeah, he threw his bike in the back of her car, hopped in the passenger seat, and *waved* at me through the window as they drove away."

I couldn't stop the growl from escaping me this time. How *dare* he? How inconsiderate of another person's feelings does someone have to be to be that blind? That *immature*? I nuzzled my nose into the crook of her neck as her sobs took over once again.

Scarlett, it's okay. It'll be okay. That guy—he's a jerk, and you deserve so much better. This will pass. It's okay, Scarlett—

I nuzzled and purred against her, trying desperately to pass my warmth, my love, through her. She needed it—she *always* needed it. Because while Scarlett Dempsey was strong, proud, and passionate, she had been knocked down again and again and again. The men she surrounded herself with were callous and selfish. They took advantage of her kindness and the care she put forth to everyone around her, everyone she cared about. She was trusting, open, and willing to give anyone and anything a second chance. But these men... they didn't deserve it.

They didn't deserve *her*.

She wrapped her arms around my neck and squeezed herself close. Her red, splotchy face pressed against the fur of my cheek. Her tears soaked into my fur, but I ignored them for now. I would clean myself later. For now, Scarlett needed my attention, my presence, and my care. Something no other person in her life had given her.

I nuzzled my wet nose deeper into the curtain of her hair and pressed it against her neck. I purred, vibrating with warmth and love for this girl before me. She had cared so much, so deeply, from the very beginning.

For every new man who entered her life, she wiped the board clean and tried again. Every time, she started with a blank slate, and every time, they hurt her. Only for her to come home in tears, crying over a man who hurt her yet again. Who let her down, who dropped her and dumped her when they found someone else who captured their interest. This perfect, loving, and gentle woman before me was hurt, and every instinct in my body told me to alleviate her ache.

But how? I could give her company; I could nuzzle her and lick away her tears with my own kisses. But that was temporary. She would welcome my help and my presence; she would cry as she hugged me and wished for better things, better people—better men in her life.

And then, days would pass, maybe even weeks, and she'd find someone new to alleviate the hurt. She would forget all about what she went through. She would jump head first into a new relationship with the promise that this one would be different. This one would be real. This one would be the last.

It never was. And inevitably, it failed, too—*they* failed her, too. And she'd come running through the door with tears in her eyes, only for me to comfort her again.

It wasn't fair to Scarlett. It wasn't fair to me.

She deserved better. And if only I weren't this animal—this furry pet of hers—I could help her. If my words weren't lost in growls and grumbles, I could talk to her however she needed. If my touches weren't contained to only nuzzles and nudges, I could comfort her however she wanted. If my soul wasn't confined to this vessel of fur and stripes, I could be the man she always hoped for.

And idea then sparked in my head as a vague memory of an overheard conversation trickled into my mind.

One summer afternoon as I lounged on the upper floor balcony of our house, I overheard two girls talking outside. They were young, maybe in high school at the time, and sat together on a bench just off the sidewalk of the dirt road.

"Come on, Bethany! Aren't you even a little intrigued that there may be a witch living in the swamp?"

A witch—? I perked up.

The other girl sighed. "Not really. Witches aren't

real, Alex. And I don't feel like wasting a whole afternoon trekking through mud to find nothing."

Alex huffed at her. "But what if she *is* real? She could use her magic to grant us whatever wish we want, just like Julia!"

"Julia was lying. She just wants the attention."

"That's beside the point. And even if Julia was just looking for attention, that doesn't explain Connor, Louis, Jacob, and Melanie all having similar experiences."

Bethany was quiet. I peeked through the railing, trying to get a better look. And just when I thought the girls might have left with the lingering silence, Bethany let out a long, defeated sigh.

"What do you even want from this supposed witch?"

"Um, I'm pretty sure you know what I'd ask for."

Bethany's tone *sounded* like she was rolling her eyes. "For Josh Martin to ask you to the dance, right?"

Alex squealed. "He's just so—!"

"Yeah, yeah, perfect and dreamy and so *cute!* I've heard it a million times."

Alex shoved at her friend. "Okay, then what do *you* want?"

"*I* don't even think she's—"

"If she *is* real."

Bethany paused for a moment, and with her pause, my mind wandered, too. A witch... living in our small coastal town? By the sounds of it, she granted wishes. If I could wish for one thing...

I looked over my shoulder at Scarlett, lounging on the sofa just inside the open door. She typed away happily on her laptop, probably talking to some new man who would only hurt her again. I flopped my head forward and set my snout on the railing. If I had one wish that a witch could grant me without question —it was easy, really. I wanted to be someone Scarlett could count on. I wanted to be a man whom Scarlett could lean on, and I wanted to show her how worthy of true love she really was.

I sat there and listened to the girls' conversation until they eventually got up to leave. In that time, I learned more about this supposed witch. She lived on the edge of the swamp, where nobody wanted to go near or intrude upon. They said the witch was fickle, and her wishes weren't granted for free. She demanded that something be taken if something else were to be given.

By the time the two girls were leaving, Alex had wholeheartedly believed that the witch was real and wanted to pay her a visit, while Bethany had dragged her friend away in the opposite direction of the swamp.

There was no way of knowing if the witch was real or not, but without other options available, I decided then and there to go find her myself. And truthfully, I didn't know where to begin, considering I hadn't left the boundaries of the house in years. Sure, Scarlett took me for regular strolls around the woods behind the house—where nobody would bother us or question the fact of a single woman living alone with a pet tiger under her roof.

But our strolls never extended into town, never even grew close to the swamp. I'd have to find a way to get there on my own if I wanted to try and put my plan into action.

Scarlett's sobs quieted, and her tears dried as her breaths came out of her in slow waves. *Good,* I thought, *she needs to rest and recuperate.*

I gently stepped out of her hold and nudged her hands back onto the couch cushions. I then dragged a blanket from the nearby chair over to the couch with my teeth. I lifted it over Scarlett's small form and tried my best to cover her with it. Once she was covered, and a look of peace settled over her face, I sighed.

Scarlett, it will be okay. I will always be here for you. Always, no matter what. I nuzzled her palm and let out a low, throaty purr as her thumb absently stroked my fur. That's when I decided for good. This was my time. This was my opportunity. And by the gods, I was *not* going to let one more weak-minded little man hurt the woman I cared so very strongly about.

I stepped into the room that Scarlett had set up to be an office. I pulled down the pamphlet on the corner of the desk, knowing it was exactly what I needed. A map. Scarlett had been looking at it days ago when she was trying to find the location of the next farmers market that was popping up. It had moved from the year before, and she needed a little help remembering where exactly the street was that it was being held on.

I grabbed the corner of the map with my teeth and yanked it onto the floor, where I gently unfolded it as best I could, trying not to use my claws but failing in some spots where the paper caught. I glanced over the colorful paper, memorizing streets, landmarks, and geographical features of the small town. My eyes flickered over the map searching... searching... until—

There!

At the corner of the town and closest to the largest inlet that created the peninsula that the town sat on, was the swamp. *DeBonis Marshland*, was what it was called here, but I knew the locals all generally called it the *swamp*. My eyes glazed over the marshland, searching for any kind of features or landmarks there, but there was nothing. Nothing was mapped past the line that marked the marshland. Nothing was supposed to be there.

Making it the perfect place for a witch to hide away from the peeping locals.

I took mental snapshots of the map and created my own mental route to the swamp. Once satisfied with my plan, I stepped back out into the living room and took one final look at Scarlett. She was sound asleep on the couch and breathing slowly. My jowls pulled at the sides, eliciting the slightest hint of a smile that I could in this body. I gave her palm one final nuzzle before stopping at the front door. I flicked the handle down with one large paw and pushed the crack in the door wider.

Glancing over my shoulder, I gave Scarlett one more look as I stood in the doorway.

I'll be back, Scarlett. And when I return… you won't ever have to feel unloved again. Not one more tear. I promise.

With that, I stepped outside and pulled the door shut again behind me, hooking my paw around the flat handle. I stepped out into the bright sunlight, streaming through the wide leaves overhead. I squinted at the light, stretching my paws on the warm stones leading to the front door.

My bodily instincts had me wanting to spread out in the rays of sun shining through. To bathe in the light and relax against the warm stones. But I pushed aside that instinct and followed the stone path to the roadway. It was a dirt road, tucked away behind thick trees and the even thicker woods, but Scarlett and I liked it that way. We were hidden back here, with a quiet space to call our own from the hustle and bustle of the town.

I stretched my limbs as I started down the road and put one paw in front of the other as I made my way to the edge of town and the line of the marshland. After what seemed like hours of walking, hiding, and lurking just out of sight of some locals, and then walking some more, the landscape shifted.

Tropical trees turned to draping limbs. Big, wide leaves turned to vines and creeping branches. Grass shifted to mud and moss. And all traces of the town and its people disappeared. It was quiet out here. The birds chirped and sang their choruses high up in the trees, and little animals shuffled and shifted in the bushes. But I was alone. Completely and utterly alone until I drew upon a shack.

It was tucked between the crook of two large, willowing trees. Its wooden panels were cracked and warped with age, and most likely from the moist air surrounding the swamp. A large, and poorly maintained, stone path led to the front door. I took a breath before stopping at the pink painted door.

The witch is real. This is it.

I lifted my paw to rap on the door, but a voice from inside cut me short.

"Just come in; you don't have to knock."

I pushed the door inward, and it gave without hesitation. I peeked my head inside and found the interior as old, warped, and natural as the exterior. It was a cute little cottage, like something out of a nursery rhyme. An old woman sat knitting at the lone table sitting just inside the kitchen. She didn't even look up as I stepped inside.

The door shut behind me with a mind of its own. I whirled at its click, muscles tense and my body ready to fight or flee. But the woman chuckled and set down her needles and string. Her ocean blue eyes met mine, and she smiled, her teeth as crooked as her broken glasses.

"Well, well. Who do we have here?" She croaked.

I swallowed once before I stepped forward into the witch's kitchen.

Chapter Two

"So, you want to turn into a human so you can keep your owner company."

I nodded once.

The old witch narrowed her eyes at me. "*Romantic* company."

Then it was my turn to blink at her. *I never said that. I just want to be there for Scarlett. To support her, to comfort her, to cherish her like she deserves.*

The old crone snickered, pouring herself another mug full of hot tea from the kettle on the table. She had talked to me now for an hour, knowing exactly what I wanted and letting me explain why I wanted her help so badly. She didn't call me crazy, nor did she question why a full-sized tiger was in her kitchen in the middle of the swamp. She understood me, and she understood my wishes. Now, I just had to convince her to help.

She sipped from her steaming mug before setting it down to drip more honey into it. "What makes you think this Scarlett wants your love and attention?"

I grumbled low and throaty at her. *She's a living, breathing creature on this planet. She wants to be loved, appreciated, and comforted, just like everyone else.*

"Yes, but how do you know she wants that from *you*?"

I barely wavered, plopping my head onto the tabletop instead. *I am her loyal pet. I know everything about her, every like, every dislike, every dream, every hope and desire, every stressor, every song that she sings to, and what makes her cry. I know her better than anyone else. I've seen what these men do to her, and I will never repeat their mistakes.*

"How do you know?" She raised her gray brows at me from over top her mug.

Because I love her. I always have, and I always will. Scarlett means the world to me, and the last thing I would ever dream of doing is hurt her. I can take care of her; I can show her true happiness. She loves me already as her pet, so give me the chance to show her what my love can be like as a human.

The old crone wavered, setting her mug down gently on the wooden table. She wrapped her fingers along the ceramic, her long nails *clinking* in a melodic rhythm. I watched them, desperately sending waves of hopefulness out into the room.

Please, I thought. *Let me help Scarlett. Let me show her what she really needs.*

The crone eyed me before, finally, her fingers stopped.

"Alright, tiger. You've convinced me."

I jumped up, my head lifting in a spring of motion. *She's going to help me. I'm halfway there!* I nearly leapt with joy at her answer, to which the old woman chuckled at me and waved me back.

"I will help you turn into a human, but that is all I can do. Winning the heart of the girl you love is a task in and of itself, but that is one you must complete on your own."

I will! I absolutely will!

"But that's not all." She met my eyes with a stony hardness in her own. "In order to give you something, I must take something. Magic comes at a price and is never granted for free. So, if you would like for me to turn you into a human, something must be taken in return."

I barely gave her a second glance. *That's fine. Take*

whatever you want; it doesn't matter! Scarlett will see me for who I really am. Finally, Scarlett will be mine.

The witch tilted her head at me. "You're willing to give up anything for this girl?"

I nodded without a second thought. *Anything.*

She shrugged and pushed herself up. "Very well. Then you, Kadri, shall be granted your wish. You will be given your humanity. And in return, Scarlett will lose her pet, her companion, and her best friend. That is my trade."

I huffed. Was she serious? Her trade was the deal we were making, anyway. If I became human, of course my tiger form wouldn't be around. That was a given. I nearly rolled my eyes at the old woman. How silly of her, wasting such a trade for something so obvious.

I lifted my head and met her gaze as she smirked at me with those crooked teeth. She waved me into her living room, and there I saw the altar before her fireplace. Bottles with unknown mixtures and poultices sat on every surface, herbs dried and fresh laid on slivers of fabric, ropes tied in knots with winding threads laid about, and a thick book sat in the middle of it all.

The woman groaned as she sat on the floor before the fireplace. She pulled out a match and held it over the logs inside, and almost instantaneously, the logs sprung up with a full, roaring fire. I winced, my instincts sensing the magic lingering and swelling within this room.

She then pulled the book closer to her, resting it on the edge of the stones. She flipped page after page until she stopped on a dried, brown page with the corner nocked with a dog ear. She ran a crooked finger down the script until she stopped on a block of text. She whispered at first, her words soft and gentle until they swelled with volume as her energy arose. The magic swelled with her and moved around her in waves—pulsing in and out, and in and out again.

Something in my chest swelled with it, sensing —*feeling*—the energy prickle the skin under my thick fur. I reared back a step as the crone chanted in tongues. She closed her eyes, lifted her hands, and crushed some kind of herbal concoction between her fingers. She sprinkled it over the book and finished with a final crack of the book's spine as she threw it closed.

I stared at her in wonder, feeling the magic energy sizzle out and dissipate all around me. But when I tilted my head to lick down my raised fur, I found my tongue to be short and my skin to be... bare.

My eyes widened before I raced to the edge of the room, where a mirror hung on the wall. I teetered off balance on two legs and nearly toppled over nothing, but as my hands slammed into the wall on either side of the mirror, I looked up. There, staring back at me with those same hazel eyes, but with a face made of golden skin, high cheekbones, a chiseled jawline, and dimpled cheeks... was *me*.

A human.

My lips curled into a wide grin, and each one of my pearly white teeth glimmered in the light. I touched my face slowly, my fingers feeling and curling around each of my features until I stopped to stare at my fingers themselves. I didn't have to bat anything with my paws anymore, or get frustrated with my inability to move or do anything with my limbs. I had *fingers!*

A loud, crackling laugh thundered through me, and the sound made me laugh even more. My voice... it was deep, rich, even if it cracked with little use.

A throaty chuckle echoed from the center of the room where the witch sat, smirking at me. I turned my wide gaze to meet hers. She studied me, her eyes slowly evaluating her work.

"Not bad. This Scarlett should be more than thrilled to see how... pleasant-looking her companion has become."

I grinned at her, taking one more look at myself in the mirror before stepping away. It was in that moment that a warm breeze drifted in from the window and made my bare skin crawl and tingle with chill. I glanced down. That was when I finally realized what the woman had studied so intently. The male human body was... strange to see naked. It was so bare... so vulnerable.

"Um, do you happen to have any extra clothes?" I croaked out, grabbing the nearest pillow to cover my lower region.

The woman pushed herself up with a laughing groan and made her way down the hall. "Now you're bashful, huh? I think I have a few large t-shirts and maybe a pair of sweatpants you can borrow." And just as promised, she returned with them in her hands.

I took them eagerly and stepped into the bathroom off the main room to change. When I stepped out again, I felt odd being so covered up. It was so unusual, so stuffy. Fur was much more breathable.

"Need anything else before you go?" the woman asked as she made her way back into the kitchen.

I followed a few steps behind, still gazing wondrously at my fingers. They were so long, so sleek. Nothing like those big paws—

"I don't believe so." I managed to get out, my voice steadily becoming stronger.

The woman plopped back down in her seat and grabbed her needles and thread. "Good, then get to it. I hope this Scarlett is happy with your decision. And I hope it was worth it."

I gave her one final glance as I stopped in the doorway to the outside.

"It will be. I know it."

The witch nodded and waved me off. "Off you go to woo your girl."

"And woo I shall." I grinned.

She shook her head, a breathy chuckle pushing at her lips. I laughed, too, and stepped outside, eager to get back home. To get back to Scarlett. I didn't want to spend one more moment away from her. Besides, I had been gone too long. She might start to worry when she wakes up alone.

I rushed back home, following the mental route that I had created in my head.

However, this time, the journey was much faster as I didn't have to avoid people's gazes and hide from the locals. I even waved to them this time around, and most of them waved back with smiles of their own.

But that wasn't where my attention laid. As I trotted up the dirt road and turned onto the stone pathway that led to our house, every nerve, every muscle, every fiber of my new body tingled and pulsed with excitement.

I lifted my hand to knock on the front door, even though I knew Scarlett would have kept it unlocked. She always did. But as I moved my fist forward, the door flew open from the inside. That was the first time I met Scarlett eye-to-eye—being not at the height of her waist, but nearly a head taller than her. She glanced up at me, her eyes red rimmed and her cheeks still splotchy. But as she met my gaze, her eyes widened.

"Um, sorry. Can I help you?" she murmured, clearing her throat.

I had to shake myself to respond. I coughed to clear the last bit of phlegm from my throat, too.

"Are you Ms. Scarlett Dempsey?" I asked, feigning innocence.

Her eyes flicked across my face. "Yeah. Who are you?"

"I'm Kadr—" I paused, making her lift a brow in question. I cleared my throat one more time and gave her the smoothest smile I could muster. "I'm Kade. It's nice to finally meet you."

Chapter Three

Scarlett raised a brow, her eyes flickering over my face. "I'm sorry, but do I know you?"

I paused; a flickering pain in my chest surprised me. I knew she wouldn't recognize me. I was human, after all, not her pet tiger. But part of me still... hoped. I was with her every day, through every breakup, every holiday, every celebration, and every fit of tears. I was at her side for all of it. Now, to see her eye-to-eye—to stand face-to-face with her with nothing but opportunity in front of us—I found a hurt lingering in my core.

She didn't recognize me. She wouldn't, but it still hurt.

I lifted a hand and scratched it through the back of my hair, a chuckle escaping my lips.

"Well, no, um, I guess you wouldn't. I'm... new."

"New?"

"Yes! I... was born and raised in this town, you see, but once I turned ten, my parents moved us all away, and I've just recently moved back again."

"Okay..." Scarlett's questioning look didn't falter. "Did we know each other before you moved or something? I don't recognize you."

My thoughts raced as I looked at her. I had to control every fiber in my body from just jumping forward and pulling her into a tight hug. I wanted to feel her against me, I wanted to hold her warmth in my arms, and I wanted to comfort her after everything she had been through. But we were strangers. Scarlett didn't know Kade. So, I had to feign the innocence of a perfect stranger.

"We did have some clubs together in elementary school, but I wasn't very talkative, and I don't expect you to remember that." I laughed easily, but Scarlett only stared. She's not buying it. I needed to move on. "Anyway, I'm in town again, and after meeting with some old friends and talking, I was reminded of you. So, I thought I'd pay a visit."

"Oh," she wavered. "I don't... remember you well. Sorry."

I waved her off, my hand flying a little too far toward her. I still needed some practice with these new limbs.

"Hey, like I said, I don't expect you to. I just—" An idea struck me like a bolt of lightning. "I was hanging out with my old friends, and they mentioned your name after Logan said he had just broken things off with you—"

Scarlett's eyes widened at that. "You're friends with Logan?"

I huffed out a dry laugh at that. "I am, or I was. We aren't the closest in our group. And frankly, after hearing how he treated you with his whole vacation plan and everything, I don't even really want to be his friend anymore."

"Oh..." Scarlett took a step forward, standing in the sunlight that shone through the thick leaves above. I took this as my cue to continue.

"Yeah. I'm sorry about that, by the way. Logan's not the brightest, and he's selfish—always wants what he doesn't have. You know the type."

Scarlett shook her head slowly. "You don't have to apologize. It isn't your fault. I just..." Her voice broke with a dry, cracking laugh. "I always seem to pick the bad ones in the bunch."

I looked at her red face, her puffy eyes, and resisted the urge to pull her close. Instead, I took a deep, steadying breath and touched her shoulder. It was a light, gentle touch and nothing more. But I hoped it helped soothe her raging emotions.

"Hey, we all do that. It happens to the best of us. Right? And don't even waste your time on Logan. Like I said, he's an idiot, and you deserve a lot better."

Scarlett glanced at my hand on her shoulder, but she didn't step away or try to put any more distance between us. Instead, she—her lips curled into the smallest, sweetest of smiles.

"Thanks. I... I needed that."

"Anytime." I squeezed her shoulder gently before dropping my hand away. "So, um, anyway, it was good seeing you again, and I'm glad you seem to be doing well."

"Yeah, thanks." Scarlett's smile warmed as the evening sun made her cheeks glow.

I didn't want to go, and truthfully, I had nowhere *to* go. But I didn't want to overstay my welcome or make Scarlett question my presence here.

"So, I'll get out of your hair now. Just wanted to come say hi again after all this time." I smiled easily as the breeze ruffled my curly hair. I turned to leave, heading back up the stone path to the road. But just as I got a few steps from it and our house would have disappeared behind the thick leaves, Scarlett called out.

"Hey!"

I looked over my shoulder. "Yeah?"

She fidgeted with her fingers, her telltale sign showing her nerves. I felt the corner of my lips twitch at that.

"Do you have any plans tonight?"

I paused, giving the illusion that I was thinking over my schedule, before turning toward her again. "No, why?"

Scarlett's fingers squeezed around the fabric of her t-shirt. "Would you want to have dinner together? You know, to catch up and stuff?"

My lips curled into a bright smile just as my chest warmed with a flood of heat.

"I would love nothing more."

And so, that's how we ended up at a local café at the edge of town. We walked there together after I waited outside the house for ten minutes so Scarlett could change into better clothes. I didn't mind her t-shirt and leggings, and I told her that, too.

But she was insistent, as usual. She came back out of the house ten minutes later in jeans, a light and flowy linen top, strappy sandals, and with the barest amount of makeup on her face to cover the red puffiness under her eyes. I smiled at her and told her she looked pretty. She blushed then, but she didn't say anything more about her appearance as we walked to the café together.

We talked about the town, its people, the never-changing traditions, and her life and family. She talked about herself easily, and though I already knew every-thing that she told me about her life, I nodded and listened with eagerness.

She smiled when she talked about her job as a columnist at the local newspaper, and the blog that she was writing on the side. She laughed when she told me stories of her and her friends' adventures on the week-ends at the beach and the surrounding coves. She gazed into the distance, her eyes shining and warm when she talked about her parents living on the other side of town with her younger brother, who was finishing up high school. And she glowed when she mentioned the very interesting fact that she had a pet tiger named Kadri.

We sat opposite each other at the table, sipping on our fountain drinks and nibbling on our sandwiches as she told me all about myself.

"A pet tiger, you say?" I shook my head with a chuckle. "That's wild. Isn't it hard to handle?"

She shook her head as she sipped on her orange soda. "No, he's calm and gentle with me. He can be a bit protective, and his instincts do take over when he's out and about with me on our walks. Sometimes he even sneaks out and disappears for a few hours on his own. I never know where he goes, but I assume it's in the woods behind my house. He loves wandering around there. It's probably the closest thing to his natural habitat."

I chuckled at that. She wasn't wrong; I *did* love the

woods. It was nice to be alone and among the quiet of the trees. It was relaxing and replenishing.

"So, he wanders off, but he isn't hard to handle?"

She set down her cup. "No. He's independent, that's for sure. But he's never been difficult with me. He listens well, he responds to every emotion I'm feeling, and sometimes I even think he can hear my thoughts. That's how in tune we are with each other." She laughed.

It was my turn to shake my head, even though a swirl of pride bloomed in my chest.

"That's really cool. I'm glad you have someone so close to stay with. Kadri sounds like he really loves you."

She smiled at that. "He's my best friend. I don't know what I'd do without him."

But I could be more, Scarlett. I wanted to reach out and take her hand. To make her look into my eyes, to see the familiar gaze that she saw every day. To recognize me, to love me like she loved Kadri.

I took a sip from my drink to cool my heated thoughts. "I, uh, didn't see a tiger behind you earlier when I stopped by."

She nibbled on the corner of the second half of her sandwich. "Mm, yeah. He's on one of his wandering adventures now. I fell asleep after the whole debacle with Logan—" I couldn't stop the smile from slipping onto my lips. She already said his name like it's done and forgotten. She was comfortable with me. She was moving on. "And when I woke up, Kadri wasn't there, and the door was open. He knows how to get out on his own, so I don't try to stop him."

"Aren't you worried at all?"

She chewed her food without an ounce of worry on her glowing face. "About what?"

"Well, that Kadri might not come back? That he could get hurt?"

She waved me off with a laugh. "Kadri always comes back. He wouldn't leave me alone for too long. And have you been listening at all? He's a tiger. Nothing local here is going to try and hurt him."

I smiled, hiding it behind the lip of my drink. I took another sip. "I suppose you're right."

We finished our meals together, with drinks, stories, and laughter flowing. Scarlett's sadness from earlier drifted away and disappeared into the night as we grew closer and closer. At some point, a band started to play, and the drinks switched from sodas to beers. I puckered my lips at the sourness of the beer. I hadn't ever had one before. But I knew at the first sip, it was not for me. How did humans drink such bitter things? And why would they *choose* to?

Scarlett laughed at my face and ordered us two coladas instead. As soon as our waiter brought them out, Scarlett sipped at hers eagerly. I stared at mine in suspicion.

"It won't hurt you," she laughed. "Try it."

"But the other one..."

She scooted my cup closer to me. "It won't taste anything like that. I promise."

I stared at it, not knowing what I expected to happen.

"Come on, you big baby. You'll like it; try it!" She laughed.

I huffed around my pout at her teasing. But nonetheless, I picked up the cold cup and slurped at the straw. A cool, baby yellow substance flowed up and into my mouth, and just as I pinched my nose, expecting the bitterness to offend my tongue again, a fruity sweetness came instead. My eyes widened as the sweet, tangy drink flowed over my tongue.

Scarlett's smile cracked wide open. "Well?"

I took another long sip, downing nearly a third of the drink.

"Slow down, tiger!" She laughed. I froze, but not because the drink tingled and numbed the front of my skull. "I know it's sweet, but it has booze in it, too. Go too fast, and you're going to regret it tomorrow."

"Why?" I slurped some more.

Scarlett tilted her head to the side as her eyes danced in question. "Have you never had a hangover before?"

I shook my head slowly, feeling the curls bounce around my forehead and ears. It was... an interesting sensation.

She snorted and took one more sip of her drink before setting it down again. "You're lucky, then."

Scarlett didn't tell me exactly what a hangover was after that. But she laughed harder and harder as one, two, three coladas went down the hatch. Before I knew it, she had paid the bill after I fumbled around my pants, only then realizing that I had no wallet, no identification, and no money to pay for anything. She didn't mind, though. She said it was her treat after getting to catch up with an old friend over dinner, which had been her idea all along.

After paying, we walked out of the café together. Well, I stumbled on my own two feet, and Scarlett acted as a giggling crutch as we made our way across the street and down the boardwalk to the beach. My legs felt like two numb popsicles with a mind of their own. Granted, I was still getting accustomed to walking on two legs instead of four, but this sensation was entirely different. How could I learn to walk on two legs if I couldn't properly *feel* my two legs? And when would my vision just... stop... spinning?

Scarlett crashed down onto the sand, pulling me along with her. She giggled relentlessly as I toppled over beside her. I barely registered the fall, and I felt no pain or the sand between my toes, a sensation Scarlett had mused about for years. Instead, I felt nothing but the cool, nightly breeze off the water, and Scarlett's warmth seeping through my thin shirt.

"I told you, you would regret it!" She giggled, pushing me back into an upright seated position on the sand.

I must have given her an odd look because she giggled even more at my gaze. Those drinks—what did she call them again?—whatever they were, were evil. Toxic, delicious, mind-controlling, sweet, amazing evil.

Without thinking, I leaned my head on her shoulder. It wasn't the most comfortable position, seeing how much taller I was, but I wasn't going to complain. I let my breaths come in and out in long, slow waves— just like the ones crashing before us.

I had never seen the waves up close before. Scarlett's house was further inland and up against the woods. She lived in one of the homes furthest from the water, and yet, that wasn't really that far to begin with. But it didn't allow us to see the ocean like so many others who had paid hundreds of thousands of dollars every year for a house on the water. Scarlett and I always preferred our peace and quiet over the beauty of the waterfront. But now, sitting here so close to the raging, pulsing ocean... I could see the draw.

Scarlett leaned her head atop mine and let out a long sigh as her muscles seemed to relax under her.

"Kade?" she whispered, her wobbling, giddy voice barely audible above the dark waves.

"Hm?"

"Do you believe in soulmates?"

I squinted at the water in the dark, my foggy mind desperately trying to make sense out of what she was saying.

"Maybe," I said slowly. "Do you?"

She didn't answer right away. But then—

"I do."

"Yeah?"

"Yeah," she murmured, her voice rising, ebbing and flowing like waves as she continued. "I think everyone has somebody. Somebody they were meant to be with—destined to be with—all along. I mean, everything has its perfect counterpart. The sun and the moon, the ocean and the desert, water and fire, earth and air, sadness and happiness—"

"Peanut butter and jelly," I murmured before I could stop my foolish tongue.

But Scarlett's body shook with her laugh. "Exactly. Everything and everyone has its perfect opposite to balance it and to keep it whole. You can't have one without the other. I think people are that way, too."

Her ideas rolled around in my mind, crashing and blistering the other foggy thoughts aside. Everyone has another—a pair.

"Who is your soulmate?" I whispered.

She wiggled her toes deeper into the sand and shrugged, making my head bob. "I don't know if I've met him yet. I hope to; I'm getting impatient."

I chuckled, that warmth from earlier creeping back into my chest once more. I knew who my soulmate was if the idea was even real. There was not one doubt in my drunken mind of who my other half was.

"I guess if I don't have a soulmate, though, the closest thing to it would be Kadri," she confessed. My heart nearly stopped beating as I felt her lips curl into a smile against my scalp. "He's always been there for me. He cares for me, he comforts me when I need it, and he's my rock, always on my side, ready for anything. He's the one being in this world that cares about me more than anyone or anything else."

She lifted her head then, and I lifted mine. We both looked at each other in the dark, and even though the moonlight was dim and the crashing waves drowned out most of the noise, I could see her eyes shine and her next words echo in my ears.

"I know he's a tiger, but if I have a soulmate, I think it'd be him." She chuckled then, her smile cracking wide open. "Isn't that just silly?"

I stared, longer than I know I should have. Scarlett loved me. She noticed all my care, all my attention. She valued my comfort and needed my presence. She loved me above all else in the world, and she knew my love for her was even greater. And now... now, I was—

Scarlett pushed herself up from the sand, only stumbling a little now. I tried to follow her lead, but my legs felt like sand in and of themselves. She laughed as she helped scoop me up as I pushed my legs as hard as I could against the shifting sand.

Together, side-to-side, shoulder-to-shoulder, and later, hand-in-hand, we made our way back to the house. I nearly collapsed on the wall beside the front door, and Scarlett giggled as she turned the handle and pushed it open. I gave her a long look, to which her bubbly, dancing gaze sobered.

"I can call you a cab," she suggested.

But I shook my head, pointing at my hip... or trying to. I had no money to pay for a cab. Realization dawned on her then, and her gaze flicked inwards toward the house. She hesitated for one moment, then two. I didn't want to push her; I could sleep outside if I had to. But the house was so warm and my clothes and skin were itchy with sand, and—

"Do you... want to stay over?" she whispered shyly, her fingers toying with her flowy top.

I nearly yanked her into a hug at that. Instinctively, my tongue wetted in my mouth as I would have given her a long, wet kiss. But I swallowed my saliva instead. That would be... inappropriate considering the circumstances...

"That... would be great, Scarlett. And probably for the best." I scratched the back of my head as I grinned. "I should have listened to you at the café."

She shook her head and stepped inside, where a light was flicked on. "Yes, you should've. Come on in. I'll get you set up on the couch."

I stumbled inside, using the wall to brace my weight. I plopped down on the edge of the nearest chair as I watched Scarlett gather blankets, pillows, an extra set of men's clothes—where had those come from?—and a glass of water for me. She excused herself to let me change and to change herself in her bedroom.

I quickly made due with the new clothes, only tripping once as I pulled on the pant legs.

When she returned, she had on her pink and white polka dot pajamas with the shorts that climbed a little too high. I wanted to pull them down further; I always did. But this time, I found myself staring.

"Cat got your tongue?" she teased. I looked up and found her smirking at me from the back of the couch. She caught me.

I cleared my throat and forced myself to look away. "Sorry. I didn't mean—you're just so—well, you're beautiful."

Her cheeks reddened at that as her fingers flew to her shirt. "I'm just in my old jammies."

"Still," I murmured, an odd heat rushing to my own cheeks. For a moment, I thought I might have gotten a sunburn, but within moments, the heat dissipated.

"Alright, get some sleep. You're going to need it. My room is right around the corner if you need me, and the bathroom is right next to it if you need that. I filled your glass there and put an Advil beside it. When you wake up, make sure you take another, okay?"

I nodded slowly and sat down on the edge of the couch.

"Good." She turned toward her room but stopped in the doorway. "Kade?"

I looked over the couch to meet her glowing eyes.

She smiled. "Thank you for today. I... I had a good time."

My cheeks heated again, but I ignored them as I smiled back. Good. She deserved it. She deserved nothing but happy bliss.

"Goodnight, Scarlett."

"Goodnight, Kade. See you tomorrow."

With that, the lights were turned out, her door closed, and I was left alone in the four walls I had grown up in with nothing but my thoughts.

Chapter Four

I awoke to something shuffling around me. It started out slow and quiet, but as I lied there, it grew louder, more desperate. I cracked my eyes open to search for the intrusion, but instead, all that consumed me was a raging headache.

An ache, furious and violent, bloomed and pulsed behind my eyes. It pounded against my skull, with each beat of my heart. I wanted my heart to stop so the pain might ease, too. I buried my face deeper into the soft fabric of the pillow. The scurrying noises around me only grew louder—more incessant. I remembered blips of the night before: the café, the drinks—the sweet drinks—the stumbling, the beach, and then falling asleep on Scarlett's couch.

I clenched my teeth so hard that my jaw popped as the noises around me rang like sirens in my ears, making the pounding in my head grow more enraged. I wanted it to stop. I wanted the room to be silent. I wanted to be left alone. I wanted this godforsaken headache to vanish—

I bolted upright, the nausea and pounding headache coming right along with me. That's when, through squinted eyes, I found Scarlett shuffling through her office. The door was wide open, and books laid strewn about everywhere. My eyes shifted to the living room around me, and that's when they widened.

Not only was the office a wreck, but the entire house looked like a storm had rolled through the inside. I rubbed my eyes, at first believing the sight to be a dream that I was still a part of. But as my vision cleared, and reality came back to me, sure enough, the storm lingered.

"Um... Scarlett?" I mumbled, my voice deeper than before.

She looked over her shoulder for only a moment before tossing yet another book onto the carpet.

"Hey. I didn't realize you were up. I'm sorry if I woke you," she said, not a hint of apology in her words. She was distracted, her hands fidgeting on anything and everything.

I scooted to the edge of the couch and tried again to gain her attention. "It's fine. No worries. Are you, um, okay?"

She tossed a book over her shoulder and paused. I froze just as she did and watched as she rushed to the window as a car tutted by on the dirt road outside. She sighed and resumed her digging.

"I'm fine. Why?"

"Well, you just seem... stressed about something." I watched her flip through a few more books before dropping them haphazardly onto the floor. Scarlett *never* disrespected books this way. She took care of her books like they were her most prized treasures.

"What do you mean?"

I stood from the couch and motioned around me at the mess. "Scarlett, we went to sleep in peace, and I woke up in the eye of a storm. What's going on?"

Scarlett dropped her last book and sighed. She gazed out the window in the office once more, and at the lack of movement, she stumbled into the living room. She plopped onto the chair opposite me, and her limbs sagged into the fabric like liquid.

"I just... you know how I told you Kadri always comes back from his adventures?"

I nodded slowly.

"Well, he didn't come home last night. I left the door unlocked for him and everything. Usually, he's back by now. He's never stayed out for this long before."

I could see the slight trembling in her legs, and the fidgeting of her fingers on the hem of her shirt. I wanted to tell her not to worry, that I was right here! But that wouldn't go over well, and if anything, she'd think I were crazy and kick me out on the spot. No, I needed to be patient, to listen, and be kind and under-standing.

I moved to sit across from her and let out a slow breath.

"Do you think maybe he just found a nice spot in the woods? Maybe he decided to stay longer than usual."

She shook her head adamantly. "Kadri *always* comes home."

"Then maybe he just hasn't yet. Maybe he's just taking his good old time." I paused, a chuckle pushing past my lips at the irony of my thoughts. "Maybe he found himself a nice girl."

Scarlett surprised me when she jumped up. "Kadri is the only tiger around. Be serious! He could be hurt out there and needing my help!"

"Hey, hey—" I stood, too, and before I could stop myself, I pulled her into my arms. She was tense at first, tight and unwilling to relax. But as moments passed, and my hand stroked her back, her muscles slowly released their tension. "It'll be okay. I'm sure he's fine, and I'm sure he'll be back any time now. You said he's independent, right? So, don't worry."

Scarlett settled in my arms, her tight, shallow breaths slowing until they were normal again. Minutes went by, and she made no move to step away, so I held her. Greedily and maybe a bit selfishly, but nothing in my body would allow me to let her go now. That was, until she looked up at me with those big, brown eyes, glowing and twinkling in the light with unshed tears. A sight that clenched my chest tight every time.

"You really think he's okay?"

I pulled her to my chest and rested my head atop hers. "I'm sure he's just fine. I promise."

"How?" she murmured against my shirt.

"How what?"

"How can you promise that?"

I paused, stroking slow circles on her shoulder blades with my thumb. I let out a slow breath and felt her hot tears staining my shirt.

"I just... know. Kadri is much closer than you think. Trust me."

Chapter Five

After a slow and quiet start to the morning, Scarlett finally started to brighten again. I took it upon myself to make her breakfast, though admittedly, I had never made any kind of food before. She eyed me when I pulled everything I thought I needed out of the cabinets in the kitchen, surely wondering how I knew where everything was.

But I swiftly shifted her attention away when I pulled out a rubber spatula.

"Do you think I'll need this for eggs?"

Scarlett raised a brow at me. "A rubber spatula?"

I nodded earnestly. I tried to remember everything I had seen her use when she made eggs herself, but the rubber spatula made me waver.

Scarlett giggled, breaking the layer of tension that had settled over the room. "What, do you plan on baking the eggs? Perhaps put them in a cake or brownies?"

I pursed my lips at her, barely concealing the smile that was breaking through.

"Hey, it was an honest question!"

She full-on belly laughed, then. "Have you never made eggs before?"

I bit my lip. "I, uh... don't have a lot of experience cooking."

"Well, we must change that. Everybody should at least know the basics."

"And what are those?"

Scarlett pushed herself up from the stool behind the counter and made her way into the kitchen. She ticked off one by one on her fingers, "eggs, spaghetti, grilled cheese, and ramen. You have to know how to make those, at the very least."

I scratched at the back of my neck. "I don't know how to make any of those. I mean—I have some idea on how to, but... I would like to not burn down our house today." I laughed before I caught my mistake.

Our house? How could I be so careless?

But Scarlett waved me off without another look. "Then let's get started."

Eggs were cracked, pans heated, butter smeared, and after half a carton of failed attempts to flip the eggs with the yolk intact, Scarlett took over. She laughed as she flipped the first egg perfectly, and I gasped—followed by a pout—at her reaction. She turned on music at some point, and we shimmied and swung our hips while the eggs fried on the stovetop.

I recognized most of the songs she played, even if I wasn't totally used to using my vocal cords to sing along to them. Scarlett sounded like a sweet, chorusing angel while I... well, I would compare my singing voice to a whining, shrill cat with pneumonia. But Scarlett didn't care. She was too kind to point out my complete lack of tone.

We munched on our eggs and toast in silence, the music a calm beat behind us as we sat at the counter. Scarlett bobbed up and down on her stool as she ate, a sure sign that she enjoyed what she was eating. I smiled around my mouthful of food, not even savoring the new tastes in my mouth because of the bubbly, smiling girl beside me.

We finished up shortly after, and I helped her clean all the dishes. Once the kitchen was spotless, and the afternoon sun shone in through the balcony sliding door, we made plans to go to the beach. I had never been, aside from our little nighttime escapade the night before. But whether it was my own faulty memory or the toxins of the sweet drinks I'd downed, I couldn't seem to recall most of our time on the beach.

Scarlett gathered up towels, an umbrella, and her music speaker while I got the sunscreen, sunglasses, and hats. Once our pile of beach goods was packed into bags, Scarlett ran into her room with a grin to go change into her bathing suit. It was at that moment that I realized I didn't have a suit of my own. I called out to Scarlett, telling her my realization, and she laughed through the closed door.

"We'll buy one from the beach shop on the boardwalk!"

"Oh, okay."

I settled onto the couch, holding the handles to both bags in my hands as I waited. Minutes went by in silence, and I found my foot bobbing on the floor in anticipation. Then her door cracked open, the hinges creaking. I looked over my shoulder as she stepped out in a tank top and denim shorts that came... very high up her thighs. She smiled knowingly when she caught my lingering gaze.

"Ready?"

I jumped up from the couch and rushed for the door. "Absolutely!"

We made our way down the dirt road to the main road leading into town. We walked block after block, easy conversation flowing between us. I knew that I had been in Scarlett's life forever, and that I knew every detail about her, but she didn't know that. She thought I was a stranger from her past. And still, her smiles, her laughter, her joy, unimpeded. It let me think that maybe—just maybe—I had a chance.

We stopped at the beach shop on the boardwalk on our way. Scarlett glanced over the t-shirts and sunglasses while I grabbed a dark blue pair of board-shorts with white palm trees on them. I paid for them —well, Scarlett did, and I added it to the list of things I needed to pay her back for—and ran into the restroom to change.

I emerged moments later, and Scarlett smiled at me, waving me toward the door. We stepped outside into the bright sunshine and made our way down the boardwalk and to the beachfront.

It wasn't terribly busy for a weekday, seeing as how most people were working or busy—Scarlett was off work every Thursday, a fact I didn't forget. Small groups of kids, elementary aged all the way to high school teenagers, roamed and ran across the sand. School was out for the summer, and the sheer unadulterated joy was not remiss. Scarlett looked for the perfect spot to put our belongings while I tagged behind at a distance. It was... beautiful here.

The sun shone brightly on the sand, warming it between my toes. The waves reflected off the rays of light, crashing and pulling and crashing again in a perfect tidal chorus. The seagulls ahead cawed and perched on benches, lingering close to the few tourists who kept their food a little too far outside their towels. Coolers marked the spots of families already settled, kids ran freely, laughing and squealing with delight. I smiled as I closed my eyes against the light, letting the warmth of the beach bathe me.

"Hey! Let's set up here!" Scarlett called.

I peeked my eyes open and found her standing some twenty feet away. Her hair blew lightly in the breeze, her smile cracked wide into a bright grin, her cheeks reddened from the heat shining down on her, and she held her wide-brimmed hat down with one hand as she waved me over. I smiled as I jogged to catch up.

I set down our bags and helped Scarlett spread out the towels with the rest of our stuff. Once she was satisfied with our layout, she grabbed the sunscreen that I'd left on one of the towels and turned toward me.

"Alright, you first."

I looked over my shoulder only half-jokingly. "Me?"

That earned me a laugh. "Yes, you. Get over here, and let me get your back covered up."

"I-I can do it myself," I faltered, becoming shy all of a sudden. Why didn't I want her to touch me? Was it because my shirt wouldn't be between us? Because she'd be touching bare skin and that... that was much more... intimate?

She snorted and yanked my arm forward so I stood before her. "You can get your front and shoulders, but if you argue with me, your back is going to burn. Didn't you learn your lesson with the drinks last night?" she teased, her brows raising.

I groaned as I turned around. "Yes, yes. You know all, and I need to trust your judgment."

"Exactly." Scarlett grinned as she fingered the hemline of my shirt. "Now, off with it! Don't be shy."

I turned to hide my blush as I slipped my shirt over my head. I swore I could hear Scarlett gasp—I *swore*—but when I looked over my shoulder, she avoided my gaze. Instead, clearing her throat and rubbing white lotion all over my back. I couldn't tell exactly what surprised her, but one look at my chest and abdomen, and I had a pretty good hint.

The witch in the swamp not only made me human —she made me a toned, muscular, and nearly *perfect* human. I flexed the muscles in my abdomen, and the individual abs twitched. I smirked and glanced over my shoulder again, only to find Scarlett's cheeks bright red as she rubbed in the lotion.

"Okay, all done. My turn!" She shoved the bottle into my hands as I turned.

I smirked as I took it and squeezed a dollop of lotion into my hands. But when I looked up, and Scarlett tugged off her shirt—and then her shorts—my eyes dipped shamelessly.

She was all lean and toned. She wasn't lanky like

those other girls she always compared herself to in high school. She was stocky, sturdy, and solid. But that made her even more beautiful to me. She was fair-skinned, and her paleness made her almost glow in the sunlight. Her bikini hugged all the right curves of her chest, and then her hips, and her hair blew across her shoulders in flowing wisps.

My breath caught in my throat. But she didn't seem to notice as she whirled around to face away from me.

"Lather me up. I don't want to burn, either." She chuckled nervously.

I cleared my throat as I started to rub lotion across her skin. It was so smooth, so soft and warm. I had wanted to touch her for years, had dreamt of the feeling, even. And now... it was almost too much to bear.

"Wouldn't want that," I said, my voice coming out more like a croak. What was wrong with me?

After a few moments of rubbing in the sunscreen, Scarlett turned, grabbed the bottle from my hands, and began putting on the rest herself. I followed suit, my eyes wandering to her perfect figure. Once satisfied, Scarlett clapped her hands together and grinned, all traces of embarrassment gone.

"Ready for a dip?"

I took one glance at the water and winced. I wasn't necessarily afraid of it; I just didn't really... like it. I was a tiger before, after all. Water wasn't out of the question in my native habitat, but I had gotten accustomed to avoiding it, now in captivity. So, while the sun shone down on us with a warm, almost blistering heat, and the sand burned under my bare feet, I still didn't find the idea of a dip all too appealing.

"Uh... I might just sit this one out. I can watch," I suggested.

Scarlett tilted her head at me, her brows knitting together with her smirk.

"Oh, my apologies. I didn't know my new friend was *scared* of the water."

"I'm not scared!"

"Sure."

"I just... don't really feel like swimming," I asserted.

"In this heat? Yeah, okay. The only reason you aren't already in the water is because you're a big ol' scaredy cat!" she teased, her smirk widening.

I glanced at the water, and then back at her. It couldn't be all that bad, right? I was human now. I didn't have to clean myself like I did when I was covered in fur. I could shower. My skin could just be washed clean. And besides, it *did* look refreshing in this heat...

"Fine!" I ran past Scarlett before she could get one more poking tease in. I heard her call after me before footsteps sounded and laughing echoed over my shoulder. But I didn't stop to look. If I stopped now, I didn't think I'd have the courage to dive in.

I sprinted closer and closer to the water, and just as

I reached the closest receding wave, the water trickled over my bare feet. I flinched instinctively, but then the coolness washed over my hot skin, alleviating the burning sensation in my feet right away. My eyes widened, and before I could question myself, I ran into the deeper water and jumped in so it covered my head.

It was strange, the sensation of being underwater. Scarlett had bathed me before in the tub when I got muddy during a particular adventure in the woods. But that was different. The water—the ocean and its energy—was all-consuming.

The waves rushed over my head one after another, uncaring that I was underneath them. The water reflected green and blue in the sunlight shining down through it. The rays of light scattered, creating fireworks in the water with bubbles rising up all around. Salt tickled my nose and burned my eyes, but I didn't close them right away.

I burst up through the surface and took a gasping breath of fresh air.

"Kade!" Scarlett rushed through the crashing waves a few feet away, the water already up to her chest. "Are you okay? You were under for so long; I thought you might have gotten sucked in under the waves."

I looked at her in silence, and once she stopped in front of me, my grin broke my face into two.

"It's amazing out here! I can't believe I never came to the beach before now! It's... it's... unbelievable!"

Scarlett looked at me with the strangest expression,

maybe a mixture of something I couldn't quite place in all my excitement. But then her smile broke, too. It wasn't wide and toothy like mine. No, it was small, gentle, and surrounded by rosy, red cheeks.

"I'm glad you like it."

Without thinking, I stepped closer to Scarlett, too close to consider any sort of personal space. I looked down at her and felt her chest rise and fall against my own. Her smile faded to something serious—something intent. My own grin dimmed as I couldn't help but focus on her lips.

"Thank you, Scarlett. Thank you for bringing me here today," I whispered.

Scarlett took a deep breath, her chest pressing against my own. "You're welcome," she breathed.

In that moment, it was just us in that vast ocean of people, of energy, of water. Nothing else that had thrilled me mere moments before was important. Scarlett had my attention now.

Only Scarlett.

But the moment couldn't last forever, and Scarlett chuckled awkwardly as she stepped away. I didn't want her to, and I wanted to pull her close again, but that felt like too much. Too soon. Instead, she whisked up a slashing handful of water right for my face. I tried to block against her assault, but was too late as the salt water splashed my face.

She laughed as she splashed me again and again, and I chased her with splashes of my own. We settled happily in the water, floating among the lulling waves after our splashing assault ended, with both of us breathing heavily and spitting out salt.

After we were thoroughly shriveled from the water, we went back to our towels, dried off, and lied side-by-side on the sand. We listened to the kids run around us and the gulls screech as they flew overhead, but neither of us minded. We lied in silence, soaking in everything until Scarlett mumbled.

"I wonder if Kadri is back."

I glanced at her to my left and found her staring up at the sky through her sunglasses. A part of me understood her worry. I hadn't ever been gone this long, and she had a right to be worried. But another new part of me was... well, frustrated. I couldn't help the feeling when she mentioned my name. After all we had done together, the truths we had admitted and shared on the beach, the fun we'd just had, the company we shared, the touches, the hugs—

She still thought of Kadri. Her pet tiger was always on her mind.

I sighed to myself as I adjusted my position on the towel. "Maybe."

Scarlett was quiet at first. "Do you really think he's okay? I mean—"

"Scarlett, we already talked about this. He's strong, independent, and he knows the woods well, right? I'm sure he's just fine."

I watched her throat bob as she swallowed. "Yeah, I guess you're right. I just... worry."

I knew she did. I knew she would, after all. And in that moment, I realized something. No matter how well Scarlett and I got along, and no matter how much fun we had together, her mind and her attention would never fully be on me alone. Not with my tiger counterpart in the picture.

Not with Kadri on her mind.

I turned onto my side and smiled at her. "I know. Now, before the two of us either get heat stroke or fall asleep here, I suggest we get going."

Scarlett eyed me. "Where to?"

I couldn't believe I was going to say it, but before I could question myself, the words flew past my lips. "To find Kadri, of course."

She perked up at that. "Do you mean it? I mean... he's *my* pet and *my* responsibility. I don't want to put that on you."

I waved her off as I sat up and began to gather our things in the bags sitting idly on the sand. "You won't feel fully relaxed or be able to fully enjoy yourself until you know that Kadri is safe, right?"

Scarlett sat up also and nodded.

"Right. So, instead of worrying, let's go into the woods behind our—*your*—house and go find him. He can't be that far."

Scarlett glanced out at the water and its waves

lapping on the sand before meeting my eyes. Her voice was softer, shyer than usual.

"Are you sure?"

I smiled as I squeezed her hand. "Certain. Now let's go before we lose sunlight."

Scarlett didn't waste a moment more as she hopped up and helped me pack our belongings. We were on our way to the house before I could second guess what I had just done.

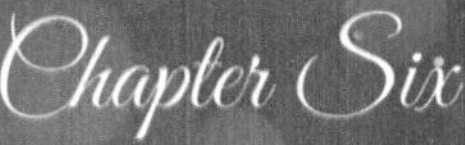

Chapter Six

As soon as we arrived back at the house, Scarlett and I unloaded our beach bags, changed into dry, comfortable clothes, and made for the woods behind the house. We walked, and walked, and walked some more. I stepped over crunching leaves, twigs snapping beneath my weight. Each little shuffle in the brush or rustle of leaves overhead made me look, but I quickly realized that my sense of hearing wasn't as sharp as before. While I was noticing this and looking for the sources of such noises, Scarlett's head swiveled, in search for her pet.

I stayed quiet at first, trying to think of a way to explain myself. Should I even tell her the truth at all? Would she believe it? I couldn't know for sure, and part of me was certain she'd laugh in my face before turning to look further for her pet. But what else was I to do? With Kadri, her pet tiger, in the picture... she would never fully accept Kade, the human. Then it struck me.

The deal with the witch. To grant me my humanity, she had taken away Kadri the tiger. I thought nothing of it at the time, but now I understood why it was a fair trade. Scarlett loved me as a tiger. I was her friend, her companion, her roommate, and so much more. The only thing I couldn't be was her lover. Now, I was human and capable of that, but in turn, she lost everything else she gained with Kadri. She wouldn't forget that.

She'd never forget Kadri. And she would never get over that loss, even with me at her side. Unless...

"Hey, are you okay?" Scarlett stopped suddenly and looked up at me.

I nearly walked right into her as I shook my head to clear it of the racing thoughts. "Um, yeah, I'm fine. Why?"

"You've been silent the whole time. Are you sure you want to help me look for Kadri? I know searching in the woods at dusk for a girl's pet tiger isn't really high up there on romantic dates." She flushed, fiddling with her shirt hem.

But I shook my head. "I don't mind. I just…" My thoughts swirled and pulsed in my mind, refusing to settle. "I want you to be happy, Scarlett."

She looked at me, and slowly, her lips curled into a smile. "I am."

"Truly?"

She nodded. "I know it's only been days, and I still have a lot to learn about you, but… it's been fun. And when I'm with you, well, all my other worries seem to float right out the window."

I smiled at that. But then my thoughts whispered again. *She might be more relaxed with you now, but she'll never forget about Kadri. No matter how long you're together, Kadri will always come first.*

I swallowed past the lump forming in my throat and stepped forward again to avoid my thoughts that came forth with the silence.

"Come on, let's keep searching."

Scarlett followed suit, and we looked up and down the woods for what felt like hours. We looked until the sun dipped, and the shadows from the trees overhead made it near impossible to see farther than a few feet ahead.

"I guess we should call it for tonight. We aren't going to find anything now." Scarlett sighed.

We turned and started heading back toward the house when Scarlett's foot caught on something. She stumbled forward, a gasp slipping from her lips. But I was quicker.

I caught her in my arms and yanked her upright again. I couldn't see her face well in the darkness surrounding us, but I could feel her eyes on me.

"Thanks," she whispered. It was then that I realized my hands still held her sides. But instead of pulling them away, I squeezed her side gently with one hand.

"Be careful. I don't want you twisting an ankle out here."

I dropped my hands away from her sides, but I didn't want to let go completely, and it seemed Scarlett didn't, either. As we started walking again, she reached out, and the backs of our hands touched. I almost apologized at first, thinking it was an accident, but then Scarlett intertwined her fingers through mine and squeezed gently. I was thankful for the darkness then, so she wouldn't see my own heated cheeks.

We walked hand-in-hand back to the house, squeezing each other's hands and pulling each other upright when we tripped over things in the dark. Somehow, we managed to get back safely and without injury, but the relief was short lived when I caught sight of Scarlett's glistening eyes as she pushed open the front door.

I followed her inside and closed the door behind me.

"Scarlett? Are you okay?" I murmured as I watched her settle on the edge of the couch.

She played with the hem of her shirt again, her eyes staring at it but unseeing.

"I don't know," she sniffled. "I want to be happy, and truthfully, I am when I'm with you. You've made me happier than I have been in a long time, Kade. But... but—"

I sighed as I came to sit beside her. "But I'm not Kadri."

She looked up at me. Her eyes glimmered with unshed tears, and her cheeks were splotchy like she could break into sobs at any moment. My chest squeezed at the expression. I knew she was worried, and I knew she was anxious, but this... I didn't want the loss of my tiger form to make her... cry...

"Hey, hey, it's going to be okay." I wiped at the corners of her eyes with my thumb, brushing away a tear that threatened to fall.

Scarlett sniffled some more. "But how? I couldn't find him or any tracks of him showing where he went. He just—disappeared!" Scarlett collapsed then, and I pulled her into my chest. Her tears stained through my shirt as they fell, but I didn't care.

"How could he just leave me?" Scarlett continued,

her voice muffled and shrill against the fabric of my shirt. "Doesn't he know how much he means to me?"

I ran a slow, gentle hand up and down her back.

"I'm sure he does, Scarlett."

"Then why?" She yanked herself away and looked me dead in the eyes. "If he knows how much I love him, then why did he just up and leave after all this time?"

I could have given her any number of excuses. He's a tiger; he's independent and needs to be on his own. He's a wild animal; he couldn't stay cooped up forever. He wanted to wander the woods because that's the closest to his natural habitat...

There were many logical reasons to explain away my disappearance, and truthfully, Scarlett would have to accept them with little other option.

But I knew. I knew that if I gave her some lame excuse, she wouldn't buy it. She loved Kadri the tiger, and even if she was forced to accept his disappearance, she would never get past it.

So really, I had *one* option; I had to tell her the truth. For her sake, for her peace of mind, and maybe to alleviate some of the guilt that had built up in my own heart.

"Scarlett, I have to tell you something, but... I don't know if you'll believe me," I started.

She looked at me, her tears slowing as she focused. "What is it?"

I didn't have a good place to start, so I went back to

the day before when she had fallen asleep after coming home sobbing after her failed date. I told her everything from start to finish. How I had heard the two girls outside the house talk of the witch in the swamp, how her sobs made me feel hopeless and wanting to do more than just comfort her as a tiger, how I decided to go find this witch to help turn me into a human so I could do just that.

I then told her how I came upon the house again, about the things that were different as a human, and how all I had wanted all along was to make her happy and to see her smile again.

"I didn't want to be stuck in the house and just be able to comfort you when you came home crying. I wanted to do more. I wanted to be someone you relied on, someone you trusted and cared about, and someone who would never, ever hurt you the way those others have." I admitted. "I wanted to be more than your companion, Scarlett. I wanted... to be yours."

Scarlett stared at me in stunned silence. Her eyes had widened and teared up as I told her everything, but not one more tear had fallen.

"You... you *are* Kadri, then?" she finally whispered.

I nodded silently, giving her a moment to soak everything in. I couldn't know what thoughts swirled through her mind. I hoped they were of relief, surprise, maybe even excitement. But what I failed to consider was that she might not be happy to learn the truth. I had kept it from her for two days while she worried about her pet's disappearance. Maybe she wouldn't be happy to learn the truth at all.

I opened my mouth to say something—that I wasn't sure. But then Scarlett cut me off.

"It was you all along. Kadri... Kade—" Realization hit as the name similarities struck her. She even chuckled. "How did I not see it?"

I swallowed past the lump that settled in my throat. "I mean, a witch turning a tiger into a man isn't a common story. I didn't expect you to realize." I tried chuckling, too, to lighten the tension.

Scarlett's eyes found mine then, and her smile slipped into a serious face. "Were you ever going to tell me? This whole time, I've been worried—"

"I know. I know you were. And that's why I needed to tell you. I couldn't stand to see you upset any longer. And when you cried..." I shook my head, the guilt festering in my chest. "The whole reason I wanted to become human was so I could make you happy. I never wanted to see you cry again. But I didn't think about you crying for me."

Scarlett's silence unnerved me. My foot bobbed, and my fingers fidgeted just as hers so often did. But I couldn't stop as she just sat there and looked over me. Her eyes skimmed up and down and up again, as if she were looking for the similarities between the me now and the me before. Just when I couldn't take the silence any longer, she sighed long and deep.

"You'll have to show me where this witch is, you know. That's a secret you're not allowed to keep."

My eyes widened. "You mean... you want her to change me back?"

Scarlett's lips slowly curled. "No. I don't."

Everything in my chest that squeezed and twisted and tightened released all at once. I couldn't stop myself as I launched at Scarlett with open arms. I yanked her into a big hug and nearly started crying myself as I hugged her tight.

"Thank you, Scarlett. Thank you. I'm so sorry for keeping this from you. I—"

But Scarlett laughed as she pulled me in even tighter. "It's okay. I forgive you. But don't scare me like that ever again, okay?"

I nodded against her shoulder, too grateful to say or do much more. We held each other for what felt like forever, but neither of us tried to move apart. It finally felt like things had settled, and the happiness bubbling up inside me welled over as relief poured in, too.

Scarlett pulled back slowly and met my eyes again. "Getting hungry?"

My stomach growled in response. Scarlett laughed at that and pushed herself up from the couch. She held out a hand and pulled me up, too.

"Let's get to it, then."

"To what?" I asked.

She stepped toward the kitchen. "Cooking dinner.

You have to learn the basics, remember? A good foundation is needed to do anything else after that."

A smile broke across my face as I followed her. She was right. I had so much more to learn, but now, with Scarlett at my side, I was ready to take on anything.

The End

About the Author

Viola Tempest is a dystopian fantasy and paranormal romance author who yearns to expose the truth of those in the modern world: the good, the bad, and the ugly. Her inspiration primarily stems from life experiences, those who annoy her, ex-boyfriends, and the crazy dreams that pop into her head every once in a while.

Stalk her below!

* * *

Website:
https://www.violatempest.com/

Facebook Page:
https://www.facebook.com/authorviolatempest

Instagram:
https://www.instagram.com/author_violatempest/

Goodreads:
https://www.goodreads.com/author/show/21693342.
Viola_Tempest

Bookbub:
https://www.bookbub.com/authors/viola-tempest

Dating the Damsel

ENCHANTED WISHES COLLECTION

VIOLA TEMPEST